This Little Tiger book belongs to:

To Holly, our wee princess
on her 2nd birthday

Lots of love Uncle Adam
and Aunt Debby.
xox.

For Matthew
~ CL

For Sven
~ GH

LITTLE TIGER PRESS
An imprint of Magi Publications
1 The Coda Centre, 189 Munster Road, London SW6 6AW
www.littletigerpress.com

First published in Great Britain 2003
This paperback edition published 2004

ISBN 1 85430 854 8

A CIP catalogue record for this book
is available from the British Library

Printed in Singapore

1 3 5 7 9 10 8 6 4 2

MOLLY and the STORM

Christine Leeson Gaby Hansen

LITTLE TIGER PRESS
London

It was the first sunny day after weeks and weeks of rain.
"Can we go out to play, Mum?" asked Molly Mouse, dancing in the pale sunshine. "Please?"
"So long as you keep an eye on the weather," said Mother Mouse.
"I'm sure more rain is on the way."

Molly and her brothers
and sister scampered across the fields.
They chased each other round hawthorn trees,
frothing white with blossom.

They hopped through
carpets of bluebells.

They were enjoying themselves
so much that they didn't notice
it was suddenly getting darker.

PLOP!
A large drop of rain fell on Molly's
nose – and another, and then another.
Big black clouds filled the sky, and
the rain started to fall faster and faster.
"We'll never get home in time," groaned
Molly. "Where can we shelter until it stops?"

Just then, a squirrel hurried by on her
way home. She stopped when she saw
the wet little mice. Her own family were
all tucked up safe and warm in her nest.
She couldn't possibly leave the mice
out in the rain.

"Come with me," she said.
"You can shelter at my place."

Squirrel ran ahead and bounded
up a tree, but the mice didn't follow.
"Your house is too high and it doesn't
look safe in this storm," sighed Molly.

An old harvest mouse popped
her head out from under some leaves.
"You can stay with me," she said kindly,
"I have a nice warm nest of twigs."

Harvest Mouse scuttled to her home,
but the mice didn't follow. They could
see that her woven nest was far too
small for them all.

"You can come to our place," cried
a little rabbit, "and join my baby
brothers and sisters in the warmth
of our burrow." She couldn't leave
these poor little mice out in the storm.

Rabbit popped down the rabbit hole, but the mice stayed outside. "Your home is very full," said Molly, peering inside at all the baby rabbits. "I think we'd all be too squashed."

Before Rabbit had time to answer, they both heard someone calling. Molly pricked her ears. "It's Mother Mouse!" she squeaked.

"Thank goodness I've found you!"
cried Mother Mouse. "The storm
is getting worse. But there's
an old hollow oak tree near
by where we can shelter
until the rain stops."

The hollow oak tree stood at the top of
a slope. The mice scrambled inside and
were soon warm and dry.
"We'll stay here tonight," said Mother
Mouse. "You can all curl up together
and go to sleep."

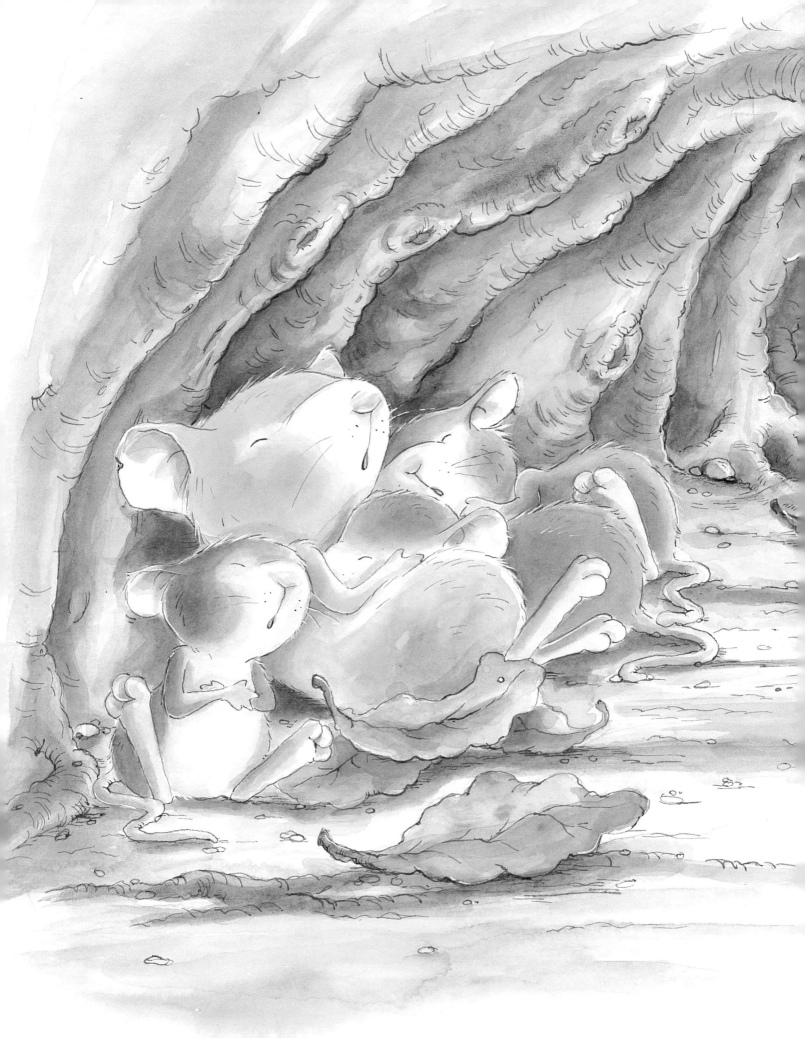

But Molly couldn't sleep. She lay listening to
the roar of the wind and the lashing of the rain,
and she was worried about her new friends.
Would Harvest Mouse's home be destroyed?
Surely Rabbit's burrow would be flooded,
and Squirrel's nest blown away? Molly looked
at her family, sleeping snugly. She couldn't
leave her friends out in the storm.

Molly hurried outside. The wind tugged and
pulled at her as she struggled across the field.
There, huddled under a swaying tree,
was Squirrel.
"You must come with me,"
said Molly. "We've
found the perfect
shelter."

Just then, looking tired and bedraggled, the
 old harvest mouse appeared out of the grass.
"Can I come too?" she asked.
"Of course," said Molly.

As they made their way back,
they passed Rabbit and
her family huddled
under a hedge. "You'll
be nice and warm if
you come with us,"
said Molly.

At last Molly and her new friends reached the shelter of the old oak tree. Outside, the wind battered the trees and flattened the grasses. But inside, everyone was safe and dry.

The wind had dropped by the time morning came,
and as the sun crept up into the sky the friends
crawled out of their burrow. There before them was
a rainbow, stretching as far as the eye could see.

"It's for you, Molly," whispered the old harvest mouse.
"It's a special present for saving us."
And Molly smiled happily, surrounded by her family
and all her new friends.

Curl up with a book from Little Tiger Press

For information regarding any of the above
titles or for our catalogue, please contact us:
Little Tiger Press, 1 The Coda Centre,
189 Munster Road, London SW6 6AW, UK
Tel: 020 7385 6333 Fax: 020 7385 7333
e-mail: info@littletiger.co.uk
www.littletigerpress.com